KU-167-394

For Gillian and Eric Hill

This mini hardback edition first published in 2017 by Andersen Press Ltd.
First published in Great Britain as *Elmer and Papa Red* in 2010 by Andersen Press Ltd.,
20 Vauxhall Bridge Road, London SW1V 2SA.
Copyright © David McKee, 2010.
The rights of David McKee to be identified as the author and
illustrator of this work have been asserted by him in accordance
with the Copyright, Designs and Patents Act, 1988.
All rights reserved.
Printed and bound in China.

1   3   5   7   9   10   8   6   4   2

British Library Cataloguing in Publication Data available.
ISBN 978 1 78344 578 3

ELMER'S
CHRISTMAS

David McKee

Andersen Press

Elmer, the patchwork elephant, smiled. It was
two days before the annual visit of Papa Red.
The young elephants were excited.
"Take them for a walk, Elmer," said an older
elephant. "Then we can wrap the presents
in peace."

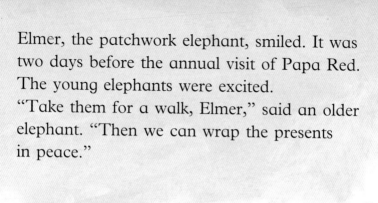

"Come on, youngsters," Elmer called. "We'll go and get the tree."
Squealing with laughter, the young elephants hurried after Elmer.

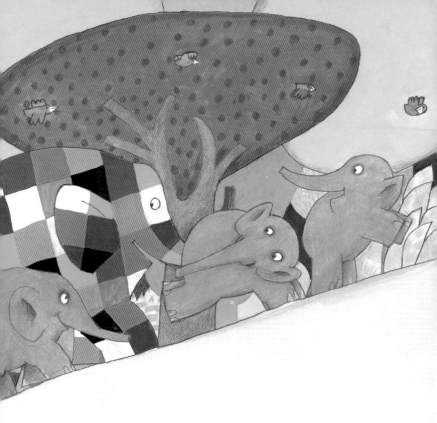

"Are we going to where Papa Red lives?" they asked.
"Close by," said Elmer.
"Have you seen him, Elmer?"
Elmer smiled. "Yes," he said. For the rest of the
walk they asked Elmer about Papa Red.

The walk went up and up. The jungle became pine trees. Then, for the first time in their lives, the youngsters saw snow. Papa Red was forgotten.

Elmer left the young ones to play in the snow
and went to choose a tree.
"Hello, Elmer," said a moose. "Let them see
Papa Red tomorrow but keep them hidden.
We'll have a busy night ahead."
"I know," said Elmer. "We won't bother you."

Elmer chose a tree that would be easy to put
back later. The youngsters helped to carry it.
By now it was late.
"Straight to bed when we get home," said Elmer.
"We have a lot to do tomorrow."

The next day everyone helped
to decorate the tree.
"The presents, the presents!"
shouted the young elephants.

The presents, wrapped and decorated, were placed around the tree. When it was finished the other animals came to admire it. "Wonderful," they said.

That night, when the big elephants
were asleep, or pretending to be,
Elmer collected the youngsters together.

"This is your chance to see Papa Red," he said.
"Hide where you can see but not be seen."

The youngsters had just hidden, when, from out of the sky, came six moose, pulling a sleigh with Papa Red aboard. They landed, and Elmer helped load the presents into the sleigh. "Thanks, Elmer," said Papa Red. Then he winked. "I'm glad we weren't seen."

Papa Red flew off.

"We saw him, we saw him!" the young ones shouted. "He took the presents."

Elmer laughed and said, "This is the season for giving. We give and Papa Red takes the presents to whoever needs them the most."

Once all the elephants were finally asleep, Elmer tiptoed among them. By each young elephant he placed a present that Papa Red had left for them. Elmer smiled. "Good old Papa Red," he said.